Books are on loan for 21 days from date of issue.

Fines for overdue books: 10c for each week or portion of a week plus cost of postage incurred in recovery.

The Not-So-Very-Nice Goings-On at Victoria Lodge
*Without Illustrations by the Author*

*by the same author*
*published by Faber & Faber*

fiction

*The Eddie Dickens Trilogy*
Awful End
Dreadful Acts
Terrible Times

*The Further Adventures of Eddie Dickens*
Dubious Deeds

*Unlikely Exploits*
The Fall of Fergal
Heir of Mystery
The Rise of the House of McNally

non-fiction

The Hieroglyphs Handbook
*Teach Yourself Ancient Egyptian*

The Archaeologist's Handbook
*The Insider's Guide to Digging up the Past*

Did Dinosaurs Snore?
100 $^{1}/_{2}$ *Questions About Dinosaurs Answered*

Why Are Castles Castle-Shaped?
100 $^{1}/_{2}$ *Questions About Castles Answered*

# THE NOT-SO-VERY-NICE GOINGS-ON
## at
# VICTORIA LODGE

*Without Illustrations by the Author*

## by

# Philip Ardagh

Illustrated with pictures taken from
*THE GIRL'S OWN PAPER*
1891–1897

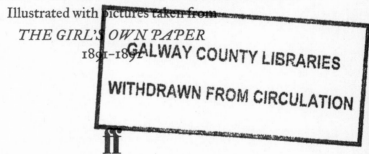
ff

*faber and faber*

First published in 2004
by Faber and Faber Limited
3 Queen Square London WC1N 3AU

Typeset by Faber and Faber Limited
Printed in England by Mackays of Chatham plc, Chatham, Kent

The right of Philip Ardagh to be identified as author of this work has been
asserted in accordance with Section 77 of the Copyright, Designs and
Patents Act 1988

A CIP record for this book
is available from the British Library

ISBN 0-571-22357-5

2 4 6 8 10 9 7 5 3 1

# WHAT YOU ARE ABOUT TO READ

One of the frustrations of an author unable to draw is that he is reliant on another (however brilliant) to illustrate his stories for him. This tale of a family under siege came about the other way around. Whilst flipping through issues of *The Girl's Own Paper* from 1891 and 1892, I gradually realised that, in the illustrations, I was witnessing tantalising glimpses of an unfolding story of mystery and intrigue that bore no relation to the actual text on the page. It was down to me to rearrange the order of these illustrations and to relate that tale in its full horrific detail. Apart from being cropped or adjusted in size in order to best fit, not one of these pictures has been 'doctored' in any way. Here, then, for the very first time, is the complete and unadulterated tale of THE NOT-SO-VERY-NICE GOINGS-ON AT VICTORIA LODGE *Without Illustrations by the Author*. I respectfully dedicate it to the original illustrators.

PHILIP ARDAGH
East Sussex

# THE NOT-SO-VERY-NICE GOINGS-ON
## AT
## VICTORIA LODGE

*Without Illustrations by the Author*

My name is Thelma, and it is the general consensus that I was very lovely in my youth.

I lived with my family at Victoria Lodge. It was very picturesque, but liable to severe weather conditions.

My bedroom was deceptively spacious . . .

. . . but many of the rooms were damp, and our hats were susceptible to fungus.

I took to growing mushrooms in my stocking drawer.

It was a rough neighbourhood and my dear papa was regularly mugged by gangs of local youths.

My tragic tale began when my eldest sister Edith was tending to the letter M in the shrubbery.

We had a number of letters in our garden and it was her duty to feed and water the consonants from J to T.

At the same time, our baby sister, Beth, was playing with an old O down near the compost heap . . .

. . . under the watchful eye of our faithful governess, Miss Pregg.

As usual, sister Lillian was drugging the hired help
with sweet-smelling herbs . . .

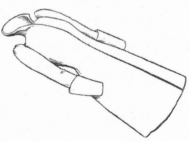

. . . and removing
all their clothing.

My mother, meanwhile, was examining a slice of
ham that my dear papa had purchased
from an exhibition in
Paris.

Suddenly, without
warning, she was
stabbed in the
bottom
with a
giant hat
pin.

Her screams brought Papa from his study and letters of sympathy from all parts of the country.

She did not see her assailant clearly, and later picked out a plainclothed policewoman in a hastily convened identity parade.

It wasn't only Mama's bottom which was spiked.
There was something wrong with the fruit and
vegetables.

Someone meant our family harm.

Later that month, my young sister, Penny, was snatched by passing twins and tossed into the path of an on-coming train.

The following week, she was playing the piano when her music teacher was shot through the window by a markswoman in a hot-air balloon.

For her own protection, Penny now carried a cleverly concealed machine gun with her wherever she went.

Lillian settled for a more ladylike miniature
baseball bat.

Out walking in the park one morning, my mother
and younger brother were almost killed by the
detonation of a nearby atom bomb.

They glowed in the dark for some weeks after that, saving us costs on both lighting and fuel.

At first, we suspected that the culprit was a member of staff and, therefore, interviewed them one at a time.

One held a grudge against Penny, after my sister had
tossed a pancake onto her head one Shrove Tuesday.

Those who couldn't account for their movements
were given a further grilling.

Papa seemed convinced that a particular young and pretty maid was somehow involved. He confronted her in his study . . .

... again, at the edge of the common ...

... on more than one occasion ...

... then at the annual charity fancy-dress ball ...

. . . and on a train to Hartlepool, where he surprised her with a false beard and a bag of lemon sherberts.

Much to his embarrassment, she managed to push poor Papa out of the compartment and onto the track.

In an effort to avoid him, she became a mistress of disguise.

As a result, we were forced to issue the staff with identity papers.

Events took a turn for the worse when dearest
Grandmama located a poorly concealed land mine
by her favourite reading chair.

The delivery of an over-stuffed robin, packed full of dynamite, was the final straw.

All incoming mail was carefully scrutinised thereafter.

Suspect packages were destroyed in controlled explosions, carried out some distance from the house.

Grandmama now refused to leave home and sat by the fire, breeding giant hamsters. She watched them exercise in a specially constructed wheel.

The kitchen staff soon became exhausted by the creatures' insatiable appetites.

Aunt Lizzy was also affected by the faceless threat to our family and home.

She took to sitting with a loaded revolver upon her lap and a box of ammunition upon the table, both concealed by carefully placed handkerchieves.

Paranoia spread. Whilst I kept gentleman callers talking, Grandmama would subtly measure the depths of their hats with a device of her own making.

She was checking for false bottoms containing concealed weapons.

Lillian also checked for false bottoms. No newcomer was safe from her body searches.

Father would lock himself in his study for hours and smoke late into the night.

I rarely left Victoria Lodge but, on those infrequent instances that it was absolutely necessary, I kept in constant contact with my family by means of a large satellite dish strapped to my back.

On one such outing, I spotted my papa buying 'tobacco' from an undesirable . . .

... and Mama choosing a new sibling for us, settling on a baby boy.

I had often suspected
her story about the stork to be untrue.

Upon my return, I found a tin of rat poison missing from my box of most treasured possessions.

On entering the morning room, I came upon my eldest sister Edith preparing a nourishing soup from deadly nightshade.

I pretended to be asleep and, unaware that I was watching, Edith slipped my tin of poison out from behind the clock, tipping its contents into the soup.

I warned the rest of the family, so the luncheon remained untouched.

In a matter of minutes, the soup tureen sprouted worrying mould.

My brother Morris went for help whilst I, disguised as a pot of ferns and foxgloves, kept an eye on Edith.

A plainclothed policewoman marched into the house and slapped the handcuffs on her wrists.

'It's a fair cop,' sighed my eldest sister as she was led from the room.

I am told that her cell was comfortable, if somewhat basic.

Little Beth wept at Edith's fall from grace.

Father aged overnight and retreated into painting.

He could draw sunrises rather well . . .

. . . and was also good at origami.

Sadly, my own efforts at paper folding resulted in little more than a crumpled mess, causing my father further distress.

I tried to cheer him up with a change of hairstyle and a little light music.

Unfortunately, this had the opposite of the desired effect. Morris tried humouring him with his party piece: an impersonation of a man of restricted growth.

The shock of her eldest daughter's betrayal turned
my mother to religion. She changed her name to
April and became a Buddhist nun.

Aunt Lizzy moved to Cyprus and developed a machine for making baby conifers.

Edith revealed the whereabouts of her accomplices; the twins who'd assaulted Penny. They were finally caught trying to flee the country on skates.

And me? I grew to be more lovely by the day, leading a quiet and uneventful life . . .

. . . until, that is, the shipwreck . . .